One Dark Night

Lisa Wheeler
Illustrated by Ivan Bates

Harcourt, Inc.

San Diego   New York   London

www.HarcourtBooks.com

Library of Congress Cataloging-in-Publication Data
Wheeler, Lisa, 1963–
One dark night/Lisa Wheeler; illustrated by Ivan Bates.
p.   cm.
Summary: Mouse and Mole feel afraid one dark night crossing a
mush-mucky swamp and a marsh-misty wood.
[1. Mice—Fiction.   2. Moles (Animals)—Fiction.   3. Fear—Fiction.
4. Bears—Fiction.   5. Friendship—Fiction.   6. Stories in rhyme.]
I. Bates, Ivan, ill.   II. Title.
PZ8.3.W5668On   2003
[E]—dc21   2001005964
ISBN 0-15-202318-6

First edition
H G F E D C B A

The illustrations in this book were done in wax pencil crayons
and watercolor on Winsor & Newton Lana paper.
The display type was set in Bernhard Modern.
The text type was set in Schneidler Medium.
Color separations by Bright Arts Ltd., Hong Kong
Manufactured in Mexico
This book was printed on totally chlorine-free Enso Stora Matte paper.
Production supervision by Sandra Grebenar and Ginger Boyer
Designed by Lydia D'moch

In memory of my good friend Linda Smith,
the bravest mouse I ever knew
—L. W.

For George, with love
—I. B.

In a wee little house,
In a wee little hole,
Lived a wee little mouse
And a wee little mole.

They munched tiny crackers.
They served tiny teas.
Filled wee tiny smackers
With wee tiny cheese.

Meanwhile...

In a BIG GIANT lair,
Near a BIG GIANT glen,
Lived a BIG GIANT bear
In his BIG GIANT den.

He growled BEASTY growls.
He stomped BEASTY feet.
He stuffed BEASTY jowls
With a BIG BEASTY treat.

Then, one dark night...

The two teensy friends
Left their wee tiny house.
"I'm scared of the dark,"
Mole whispered to Mouse.

"There's no need to fear,"
Mouse said with a sigh.
Then the moon disappeared
Behind clouds in the sky.

Meanwhile . . .

In the BIG GIANT lair,
Near the BIG GIANT glen,
The BIG GIANT bear
Stomped around in his den.

He peered out the door.

He tramped and he paced.

He craved
something fresh
With a rich,
meaty taste.

Meanwhile...

With a SQUISH-SQUASH-A-SQUISH
And a TROMP-TRIP-A-TROMP,
Mouse and Mole trudged
Through the mush-mucky swamp...

Under sharp thistle thorns,
Into marsh-misty wood,

To the BIG GIANT glen
Where a gnarled oak stood.

Meanwhile...

The bear licked his chops,
Heard his BIG tummy groan.
"I'M HUNGRY!" he roared.
But he waited. Alone.

"We're lost!" shouted Mole.
"Don't fret," the mouse said.
"I'll climb up this tree
And spy what's ahead."

From tree trunk to branch,
Mouse pushed to the top.

Fragile twigs snapped.
But Mouse didn't stop.

"What do you see?"
The teensy mole cried.
"It looks like a cave—
With a light on inside!"

From deep in that cave
Came a BIG GIANT growl.
"I want something to eat
And I want it NOW!"

Bear threw open the door,
Stomped out of the den,
Bared BIG sharp white teeth,
And charged into the glen.

Mouse perked his ears.
Heard SNARL-SNUFF-A-SNUFF.
"SOMEthing is coming!
And that SOMETHING sounds tough!"

Mole shivered. Mouse shook.
Their fur stood up straight.

The SOMETHING was Bear,
Who grumbled . . .

"YOU'RE LATE!"

Then they skipped hand in hand,
From the glen to the lair,
For a BIG GIANT feast

With their best friend BIG Bear.